STAR WARS ™

AT-AT ATTACK!

WRITTEN BY CALLIOPE GLASS
ART BY PILOT STUDIO

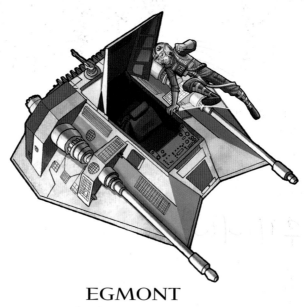

EGMONT

We bring stories to life

First published in Great Britain 2016
by Egmont UK Limited, The Yellow Building,
1 Nicholas Road, London W11 4AN.

© & TM 2016 Lucasfilm Ltd.

ISBN 978 1 4052 8366 3
63761/1
Printed in Singapore

To find more great *Star Wars* books, visit www.egmont.co.uk/starwars

Stay safe online. Any website addresses listed in this book are correct at the time of going to print. However, Egmont is not responsible for content hosted by third parties. Please be aware that online content can be subject to change and websites can contain content that is unsuitable for children. We advise that all children are supervised when using the internet.

The planet Hoth
was very, very cold.
Nobody wanted
to live there.

It was the perfect place for Luke, Han, Leia and the rebel army to hide.

They were hiding
from Darth Vader.

Vader sent robots into
space to find the
secret rebel base.
One of the robots found it.

Vader sent his AT-ATs
to attack the rebels.
The rebel base was
not safe any more.

Princess Leia
told all the rebels
to fly away.

But she chose to leave last
to make sure the rebels left
safely. Han and C-3PO
stayed with her.

Luke wanted to protect the base. The rebels needed time to escape.

Luke hopped into
a fast ship.

He flew out
to attack the AT-ATs.

The AT-ATs were strong.
Luke tried shooting
at them, but
nothing happened.

While Luke fought the AT-ATs,
Han, Leia and C-3PO
ran to Han's ship.

But Han's ship was not working.
The motor would not start.

Leia was annoyed.
She thought Han's ship
was a bucket of bolts.

Han and his friend Chewie
tried to fix the ship.

They were running
out of time.

Luke needed to
stop the AT-ATs.

Luke and his friends
used cables to trip an AT-AT.

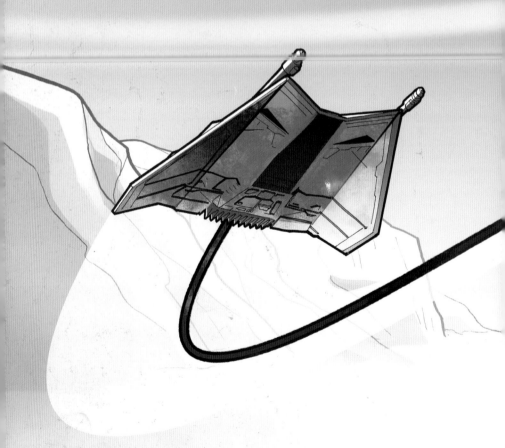

The AT-AT fell down.
Then it exploded!

Luke used
his lightsaber
to stop another AT-AT.

Luke had saved the day!

Darth Vader arrived
at the base.

Vader and his troops
fired at Han's ship.

But at the very last minute ...

... Han's ship
finally started.

Han and Leia flew away.
Luke saw their ship escape.
Luke smiled.
They were all safe!

Their base was destroyed,
but the rebels had
escaped to fight another day.